Mary F. Cusack

Jim Carty's Trial

Mary F. Cusack

Jim Carty's Trial

ISBN/EAN: 9783337405458

Printed in Europe, USA, Canada, Australia, Japan

Cover: Foto ©Andreas Hilbeck / pixelio.de

More available books at **www.hansebooks.com**

TIM CARTY'S TRIAL;

OR,

Whistling at Landlords.

A PLAY FOR THE TIMES.

BY

SISTER MARY FRANCIS CLARE.

(THE NUN OF KENMARE.)

NEW YORK:
STEPHEN MEARNS, PRINTER.
73 Barclay Street.

1886

INTRODUCTION.

I HAVE been asked many times during the last few years, to write some Plays, for use in Colleges, Academies, and Convent - Schools. Several others are in preparation. The present Play is especially suited to passing events, and a little Comedy may not lessen the value of the information which it conveys, on the important subjects which so deeply affect the temporal and spiritual future of the Irish race.

As some of the speeches are too long for acting, I have published a cheaper edition in which they are very much curtailed and the appendix omitted.

SISTER M. FRANCIS CLARE,

Sisters of Peace,

78 Grand Street, Jersey City, N. J.

Dramatis Personæ.

LORD DRIVE-EM-OUT, Irish Landlord who lives in England.

MR. EVICTEM, Lord Drive-em-out's Agent.

FATHER O'SULLIVAN, Parish Priest.

TWO SISTERS.

* TIM CARTY, boy of six years, who whistled at a Landlord.

MR. HAPPYROCK (Gladstone).

LORD STOPPER (Cork).

EARL OF UPLANDS (Lansdowne).

DUKE OF KILTENANTS (Devon).

SIR LITTLE EMLY.

SIR VERY VERY (de Vere).

LORD CORNINGHAM.

MR. JUSTICE, (wish-to-be Lord Chancellor.)

MR. WILEY, (wish-to-be judge,) Q. C.

MR. COSTS, Solicitor.

MR. FEARLESS, Counsel for the National League,

MR. ROCK-RENT-EM, J. P.

TIM O'SULLIVAN.

THOMAS BROWNRIGG.

JAMES McCARTHY.

JOHN MOLONEY.

    Police, Judges, Jury, Crowd of Tenants, etc., etc.

---

* A child was really tried in Ireland for whistling as a landlord passed by.

NOTE.—A great deal of capital was made for Irish landlords, because of the alleged inhumanity of the Irish to dumb animals. *Inter alia* a few hairs were pulled out of the tail of a pet donkey, belonging to Lord Lansdowne's children.

TIM CARTY'S TRIAL,

OR ;

Whistling at Landlords.

ACT I.

SCENE.—*A rent office. Maps of the estate hung on the walls. Landlord maps of Ireland, showing how much they own, and how little the people own. The table scattered over with lists of tenants who are to be evicted, or to have their rents raised.*

Enter Landlord, LORD DRIVE-EM-OUT. *He takes up a newspaper in which he finds a report of a Land League meeting at which the fourth "F" has been suggested to landlords—"to fly." Looks at it. Crushes it in his hand, flings it on the ground, and commences to soliloquise.*

LORD DRIVE-EM-OUT.

To fly, or not to fly, that is the question:
Whether 'tis safer to suffer in the purse
The loss of rent, and these outrageous land leaguers,
Or to defy this sea of meetings, and, by opposing, end them;
Or by coercion, or some other means, to gain the victory?
Alas ! alas ! this is a consummation devoutly to be wished.
To fly, to go—but then, to have less money—there's the rub;
For in my English home what needs I have,
For in that home what calls may come

When I have shuffled off these men.
For who could bear their land league gibes and taunts,
Their hate of landlords, and their scorn of rents ;
Their insolence of power, and the wild way they flout
All our past care of tenants.
Better, perchance, to fly, when rents have ceased,
Into some other country—(could I find it)—
Where I might quickly extirpate the race,
As my forefathers did in Erin.
Or shall I bear the ills I have, and even Parnell,
Or dare meet others that I know not of.
Alas ! I think betimes our greed makes robbers of us all.

(*Enter land Agent with obsequious bow.*)

Mr. Evictem. My lord, I interrupt your lordship. Your
lordship's tenants await your lordship's will.

(*Soft whistling heard outside the windows. Tune : "The whistling
thief."*)

Lord Drive-em-out. (*Turning to Agent with threatening looks*).
Pray sir, what does this mean, sir ? Am I to be whistled at, on
these—ahem !—rare occasions on which I visit my estate ?

Mr. Evictem. Some boy, my lord ; some thoughtless boy.
Indeed, indeed, my lord, since your lordship's land league—I
mean the land leaguer's lordship—in fact—

(*Whistling grows louder, and some shout defiantly outside.*)

Lord Drive-em-out. This is in-tol-er-able, sir. If you are
not shot instantly, as you would have been long ago, if you
had managed the estate properly, I will get another agent, sir.
I *must* have order.

(*Whistling, joined in by several boys, grows louder still—more defiant —noise of a crowd outside.* LORD DRIVE-EM-OUT *looks rather nervous —moves about—gets near a window to look out—stares back at some sudden noise—*).

(*Noise outside like a revolver shot.* MR. EVICTEM *shows symptoms of fear.*)

MR. EVICTEM. Better be quiet, my lord. I assure you, my lord, times have changed; old manners, you know, my lord, and all that kind of thing: though, indeed, the *Times* does say, my lord—

(*Singing outside, one man's clear voice, sings :*)

> Oh ! no, we never mention it,
> The name is never heard,
> Eviction, for excessive rent,
> Is a forgotten word.

LORD DRIVE-EM-OUT. 'Pon my honor, sir, this is a nice state of things, a very nice state of things.

MR. EVICTEM. My lord— I think, my lord, you had better pacify them. I assure you, my lord, its all that confounded land league, and those returned Americans, my lord. They're a bad lot, and worse when they come home ; though, of course, they could not come home if they had not gone out. You see, my lord, these Americans have such ideas of independence, they actually think a man right to have some profit for himself from his farm—

(*Loud voices outside :* Three cheers for the land league, boys— *loud cheering*—three cheers for Davitt—three cheers for Parnell— three cheers for old Ireland—and groans for the bad landlords— *awful groaning.*)

MR. EVICTEM. My lord ! my lord ! you had really better see

them. They only want you to lower their rents, but they will
not pay more than Griffith's valuation; and, after all, my lord,
you know you might do it just for one year. There's your rent-
roll: £60,000 a year, from your Kerry estate; £20,000, from your
Meath estate; £40,000, from your Limerick property; and, if
you take off what you put on over Griffith, you will still have
nearly £60,000 for your expenses in England and on the Contin-
ent. You might as well promise anyway, and get safely out of
this.

LORD DRIVE-EM-OUT. And, pray, where am I to get money
for my race horses, and to keep up my stud; and, do you know,
sir, I am master of the hounds in the county in England where
my smallest property is, and it costs me £10,000 a year to keep
that up. And, if my Irish tenants don't pay for it, who is to
pay for it? Just answer me that, sir. The lazy hounds—I mean
the lazy Irish. Sir, my hounds *must* be well fed; and they cannot live on potatoes, sir. And, then, the parson of the parish in
England expects me to give coal, and blankets, and soup, and
flannels all the winter round, and where is the money to come
from for that, sir, if I am only to get Griffith's valuation from
these lazy blackguards. Evict them, sir! evict the whole of
them! clear the country, sir! Do what Cromwell did, sir! He
knew how to manage Ireland, sir!—

MR. EVICTEM. But, my lord—

LORD DRIVE-EM-OUT. But me no buts, sir. It's the butt end
of a musket they want, sir, or buckshot, sir, (*smiles grimly*).
Foster's a clever fellow, sir; clever fellow—member of the So-cie-
ty of F r i e n d s, sir; wanted to shoot them easy and mercifully,
sir; against his conscience to kill, sir; but killing is no murder
when it's done in Ireland; soothed his conscience, sir, by pro-
fessing to do it the easiest way; bullets sounds hard, you know,
sir; too rough for a peaceful 'f r i e n d,' but buckshot, sir; quite
a new easy remedy for Irish complaints; showed such good feeling, you know, sir, to let them die easy—

MR. EVICTEM. But—I mean, if you please, my lord, some of them *can't* pay their rents—

LORD DRIVE-EM-OUT. Who said they could, sir? What do I care—you understand me—I *must* have my rents.

(*A loud knock at the rent-office door.* LORD DRIVE-EM-OUT *looks alarmed.*)

MR. EVICTEM. You need not be afraid, my lord. I assure you the people are very quiet. The priests won't allow them to commit any outrages. We had real difficulty to make up any for the papers, only for your donkey's tail, my lord—I mean, the tail of your donkey—

(*Another loud knock. A boy opens the door and peeps in; runs out again.*)

MR. EVICTEM. Only for that donkey, my lord, I don't know what we'd do. Told so well with the English public, ha! ha! ha! Why, you, sir—I mean, my lord, every hair of that tail was worth its weight in gold. Heard one of those nuns, who's been demoralizing your lordship's tenants, by feeding them, got a letter from an English gentleman to know was it true. Stopped the supplies, my lord, at once. Could not think of helping such a vile lot. Could not think of feeding men who would hurt a hair of the tail of your noble lordship's donkey. Well, sir—I mean, my lord, it was the best outrage ever happened— told so well—English papers full of the base ingratitude of the people for whom—ha! ha! ha!—your lordship had made so many sacrifices—had even come to live amongst them—of course you can never come here again. We got a house burned down after; but it did'nt do so well—wanted the touch of sentiment that made up the donkey's tail—lordship's children, you know, and all that—

LORD DRIVE-EM-OUT. What do you mean, sir? about my children being donkeys? You don't know what you are saying, sir. You are presuming! What donkeys, sir?

Mr. Evictem. My lord, I humbly ask your lordship's pardon and the donkey—I mean the children's, my lord—would not have touched a hair of his tail, sir, but, you know, my lord, we should have an outrage to get the place proclaimed, and the children's—I mean, my lord, Petty—petty—and Lady Ellen Petty's donkey told so well—so inhuman, you know, to ill-treat poor dumb animals, and, above all, a donkey that the children—I mean, my lord,—and the young my lady rode. Anyway, it stopped the relief, my lord ; you know it did. You know the English gentlemen who were sending help to the nuns here stopped it at once. The nuns couldn't deny, you know, that, for once, anyway. Couldn't go on, you know, my lord, with evictions, and all that, while the people were starving, and you know they were, my lord—

Lord Drive-em-out. I know nothing of the kind, sir, It was not their business to starve. Treated so well, too, as they were, and all the time I was getting money to give them employment from the government, and they would not take it—would not improve their farms at their own expense. I will write to the *Times*, sir ; and take care that English people shall know what they are. Hear them now out there. I must have the riot act read. Get the police, sir! We want more police, sir! Telegraph to-night to the castle and say my life is not safe here! I'll have no nonsense, sir! If you are shot I can get another agent quickly enough in your place, but who is to fill *my* place, sir ; answer me that, sir ?

(*Enter 7 or 8 respectable farmers. One is being pushed forward a little by the rest. A voice just outside is heard singing :*)

Song.—How the British Lion Roars.

How the British lion roars,
Except when he's near the Boers,
And then he sings so small,
    Ha! ha! he! he!

And he says you are so strong,
I'm sure I'm in the wrong,
I ask your pardon with humility,
I ask your pardon with humility.

When you fight, I cut and run,
But I never see the fun
Of giving in to people who are weak,
    Weak, weak.

For never, on the strong,
Could I think of doing wrong,
I have far too much humility,
I have far too much humility.

Candahar I could not keep,
Though I bought it once so cheap,
And only lost my honor and my crown,
    Crown, crown.

And that wicked man, Parnell—
Oh! who can ever tell—
How I cannot sleep for thinking
Of his plans, plans, plans.

    (*Enter crowd of Irishmen.*)

1st Man. Och! go back!

2nd Man. Spake up, man!

3rd Man. Tell his honor the truth!

4th Man. *His honor*, faith ye may go look for it! if he ever
.d any. he's left it after him in England.

5th Man. Costs too much to bring it across the say.

1st Man. Ah ! go on, man !

5th Man. Faith he might carry it with him all day and not feel the weight—

1st Man. Hould your tongues, boys. Mike's speaking up illegant to him. I gave him a glass of Guinness' stout afore he came in—

2nd Man. Thrue for ye, and shure it's the only stout thing in all Ireland—

1st Man. Oh ! boys, do whist !

3rd Man. Ah ! bad manners to ye, ye villains, and ye'r talk about the stout. That same built the Protestant church in Dublin—

2nd Man. Which, man ? the porther, or the manners ?

1st Man. My lord, we come to ask our rents—

Lord Drive-em-out. (*Aside*). That's just what I want, if I could only get it from the blackguards.

1st Man. But, my lord, you know the bad years we have had, four years, my lord, one after the other ; and its hard on them that has a family to keep—

Lord Drive-em-out. And, pray, sir, what have I to do with your family ? Its your rent I want, sir, your rent !

1st Man. Shure, your honor, we know that, and its early and late we worked to give it to your honor, my lord, for many a long year, but I have eleven of them, my lord—

Lord Drive-em-out. Go, drown them in the bog-hole, then.

Note.—The speech used on this page by a landlord to a tenant who pleaded his large family as one cause of non-payment of rent was actually made.

2ND MAN. What! my lord, to take the life God almighty gave us to keep—

[*The men shrink back in horror.*

1ST MAN. Faith, that's enough for us, my lord.

2ND MAN. The Lord have mercy on us. Does he believe there's a God at all, at all?

3RD MAN. Och! then, shure he's as good as committed eleven murders, but shure the quality can do anything. God help us!

4TH MAN. Shure its no wonder there's all them murders in England; when they hould life so chape, killin' childer comes handy to them.

1ST MAN. Och! holy Saint Patrick, what did we ever do to get them English over us?

[*All retire to the back of the stage.*

(*The priest enters and addresses* LORD DRIVE-EM-OUT.)

FATHER O'SULLIVAN. My lord, will you not even listen to these people? They dare not enter the rent office to ask for a reduction from your agent, who says (*he looks at* MR. EVICTEM,) you will not allow one farthing. Do you not know that these poor people would have died of starvation last winter only for public charity, only for munificent America? You may not be ashamed to live on public charity, but they are ashamed.

LORD DRIVE-EM-OUT. And, pray, Mr. O'Sullivan, is this (*with a sneer*,) the morality you teach your people, to refuse to pay their lawful debts. It's a contract, sir; a contract. I have kept mine and they must keep theirs. They are an idle lot, and want to live on charity.

FATHER O'SULLIVAN. The taunt comes well from your lordship. Pray, what do you do to earn your bread? and, pray, on whose charity are you living? You are living on the charity of the Irish in America, my lord; you dare not deny it, and if you had one spark of manhood you would be ashamed. You get some £60,000 a year from your tenants here; and, pray, where do they get it to give you? Well do you know that you are living on the hard earnings of the Irish girls in America; of poor girls and boys who send home their money to pay the rent for their fathers and mothers; and what matter if you even spent it in Ireland. You know well you only come to Ireland to get your rents, and perhaps to save expenses, that you may have more money to spend in England, on your pleasures and on your fashionable friends. If men like you could know shame, you would die with shame to be living on the public purse.

(LORD DRIVE-EM-OUT *walks about and gets excited during the latter part of this speech.*)

LORD DRIVE-EM-OUT. Nonsense, nonsense, sir! They take my land, and they have a right to pay me for it.

FATHER O'SULLIVAN. A right to pay you, my lord, and when did they ever deny that right, and refuse to pay you, until they had no money to give. Have a care, my lord, you are quarreling with God now, not with man. If He withholds the sun and sends the tempest, how can they reap such a harvest as will pay you. God is on the side of justice, my lord, and if you expect from the poor what God has not given them, you are not on the side of justice, or of God.

LORD DRIVE-EM-OUT. It's no use to talk any more. I made a contract with them.

FATHER O'SULLIVAN. You made a contract with them, so did the devil with Eve. Your pardon if I use strong language. There are times when truth must not be dressed in courtesies. In sooth, truth dressed in courtesies is often smothered lies.

You made a contract with them ! my lord. Such a contract is
made by force and fraud with famine and despair. When choice
is absent, contract must be void. Oh ! what a record of black
crime men go to hell with, who rob the holy poor. Let them
disguise it as they may, God sees the naked truth. I pray, my
lord, are you their only debtor ? How sickening is this cant of
honesty and contract. *You* know well the honesty you want
from your poor serfs. It is to give their all to you, and deny
their other creditors. It may do well for this world, but scarce-
ly for the next. You English, once gave us a new religion,
which suited well your lusts. Scant talk there was of contract
then, indeed ; you broke your every contract with your God.
And then you came to Erin, and did your evil best, by fire, and
sword, and famine to make us do the same. And now, forsooth,
you'd have us learn a new morality : to pay the landlord all, and
leave the honest trader ruined and defrauded. I think you
know, my lord, we would not have your faith, and now we
must decline your morals.

LORD DRIVE-EM-OUT. My contract comes first, sir. I assure
you, I want to keep on terms with the priests, if I can. Now, in
England, it is fashionable. The Catholic papers are quite full of
this subject. There's the *Catholic State*, sir ; the paper of quite
the fashionable classes, the— ahem !— few Catholics who are
cultured ; and it quite takes our side. Says landlords should be
paid in full, every penny, sir, and before all other creditors, no
matter who they are : goes on theological grounds, sir, and contract, and all that. You know, sir, when Mr. Happyrock and
other fellows wanted to stop the evictions in the—a—time, you
thought—said—I mean last winter—ah—that there was distress
in Ireland, *all* the English Catholic peers came to the House of
Lords and showed their good feeling by voting against you ;
most of them had never voted in the House of Lords before, in
fact, they rarely ever come there for any purpose. But they felt
a great principle was at stake. Their social position in England
required they should show how they disapproved of all this nonsense about distress, and— and— all this dishonesty.

FATHER O'SULLIVAN. I am quite well aware of it, my lord. It may happen that I know a good deal more than your lordship does about this matter. I know, for i have seen the letter, that even some English Catholics tried to prevent help being sent to Ireland in her hour of need, even while they were getting thousands upon thousands from their fashionable penitents for a wealthy church in London. I know, too, that the same fashionable Catholics did their best to make the distress appear as trifling as possible. It was not quite convenient to believe it; while they admitted that Catholic ladies were lying awake at night, wondering how they were to get money, to pay for their costly dresses and jewels. But, I think, my lord, they are bad guides for you. We have heard a great deal of talk about the conversion of England, but we have seen much of its effect in Ireland.

We hear English Catholics talk, and we know they write, as if they had a special mission to regulate every affair in the world and especially in Ireland, as if the soul of a lord or a Protestant clergyman was of more consequence than the souls of thousands of our poor people. Perhaps if these great supporters of Irish landlord oppression talked less like men of the world and acted more like Christians the conversion of England would not be so far off.

LORD DRIVE-EM-OUT. Oh! well; you know, it would be better for the priests to pull with the landlords. You see, in England, they go quite with the upper classes. I assure you, Mr. O'Sullivan, in London the churches are so magnificent: not like your wretched hovels here.

FATHER O'SULLIVAN. Perhaps, my lord, we worship God as well in the wretched hovels, as you are pleased to call our Churches. I admit they are such too often in country places. Our people are too poor to build better ones; and these wealthy Catholics, though they pride themselves on their own Churches, will do nothing for us. And, I know well, in England, how our poor people are scorned and despised if they go to the Chapels of the great English lords. We wonder little when we hear in

Ireland of so many converts who have apostatized, and of so many fashionable Catholics who make mixed marriages ; but, my lord ; we have other work to do in Ireland. We may not be fashionable, or please the fashionable world but we keep our ancient faith.

LORD DRIVE-EM-OUT. Oh! you can't expect me to like the Irish. I know they don't like me ; hate me, in fact.

FATHER O'SULLIVAN. My lord ; you might have won their love for half the pains you took to earn their hate, and it would have served you better. You babble of ingratitude. Ingratitude, forsooth ! I pray you, say what you have done to merit gratitude. What word, or look, or act of yours, has shown your love for them. They are but men ; and you, forsooth, while still reviling them, demand that they shall act like angels ; shall love you, serve you, give their lives for you, who hate them, like foul fiends. A truce, my lord, to all this folly ; or ere you dream, a stern, sharp end may come. You talk with scorn of these uncultured hinds. I pray you, sir ; what has your culture taught you ? If it has taught you mother-love, then let me quote a line from classic sources : Plautus says, that "the god's mills grind slowly, but exceeding small." Slowly, indeed ; does retribution come for sinful deeds, or else those men who rob God's poor were damned in the act.

Do you read Shakespeare, prince of poets, pride of English bards ? He says : "The quality of mercy is not strained. It droppeth like the gentle rain from Heaven upon the plain beneath." I mean no idle quibble here, my lord ; but all the rain of mercy that we get from you is raising rents. The patient tiller of the barren earth must wait upon the rain of Heaven. But you, my lord ; will wait neither for God nor man.

Such is your hateful greed for gold, you pass the craven Jew ! He asked but flesh and blood ; but you have strewn the grave-yards, and the Atlantic caves, with bones of men all exiled from their homes, because they would not make the barren earth yield all you chose to ask.

Nay, I would ask, where shall the limit be ? At every turn of
life you raise the rent. Are all times then so prosperous ? How
comes it that we never hear of a reduction ? Are seasons all the
same; do cattle never die ? Are there not sickness, or plagues,
or blights, that touch the poor man's purse? Are you to be his
God, and bid him make for you gold out of nothing? For
shame, my lord! Is England christian still ? Does she believe
the bible ? Once it was her boast to be a bible-loving race. But
love doeth what love teacheth. If you love your bible, I pray
you, do but what it asks. How says the great Apostle, James?
You know his words. That "judgment without mercy shall be
done to him that hath not mercy done." Where was your mercy
in the famine time ? *I* ask you now ; one day you will be asked
by God and all His angels! You tell us you love faith, and
boast old England sends the light of truth to all the world. I
ask you where are your good works, and still I quote that book
of which you say you read so much—of which we only ask that
you will keep its precepts. 'Twould seem, in truth, as if the
great apostle never dreamed that man would do as you have
done. How sternly he condemns the men who say to sister or
to brother: "Go in peace ; be warmed and filled, and gives
them not the food or clothing that they need ;" but you, my lord,
not only do what he condemns but add to it the further crime
of asking from the naked, raiment ; from the starving, food.
Who finds your costly fare ? Who finds the raiment rich, the
jewels that you give not always to the pure? 'Tis true, you do
not kill them. You only drive them from their poor, poor
homes. The homes they love too well. Do you believe in God,
or heaven, or hell, or in this bible ? (*He points to one conspicu-
ously placed on the office table.*) Did you give bread or clothes to
these poor people when they starved ? Or, did you, at best,
content yourself with " wishing" they were fed and clothed ?
You know, you dare not give your English dogs the food you
give your Irish tenants. Go to, you say, make money for my pleasures, I will give no straw nor help ; reclaim my land, I'll pay
you with ejectments ; till barren rocks, I will reward you with a
writ. Were you not made to starve and toil for me, your master?

[*He pauses a moment.*

(*The Gloria in Excelsis or some sacred music might be sung here by a distant choir, at the conclusion the priest goes on.*)

Hark! hark! my lord, I hear the solemn chants. The gentle Nuns doing what you have left undone for God and man repair your crime. But yet, they cannot stand for you in judgment, for each must answer for himself. These Nuns have fed the poor whom you have robbed. These Nuns have clothed the naked whom you stripped—yes, put it as you will, the crime is yours. You claim the land as yours, the people as your serfs. Then, if you claim them, feed your serfs, and clothe them.

LORD DRIVE-EM-OUT. I listened to your long discourse, though there is little reason in it. These people are the robbers. I am not; and all your charge is wasted on me.

FATHER O'SULLIVAN. My lord, I never hoped my words would have effect. But, in virtue of my office, I must use them. If you will not obey your God, can mortal hope for hearing? You say these men have robbed you and you write your miserable tales of falsehood to an English press, where you know none are to contradict you. There you are the judge and jury, and the verdict given all in one. How these men can rob you, when they do not give what they do not possess, passes my comprehension. Why, what is left to them but life, and well you know, my lord, how many lives were sacrificed upon the altar of your greed— but I have done : I see that speech is useless. Too long these men have given you what they should have kept to feed and clothe their offspring.

(*Enter* TWO NUNS *in haste.*)

1ST NUN. Oh! father; come.

2ND NUN. Come, come in haste. Two women by the way-side flung are dying. Two men are lying faint with loss of blood.   [*The priest hastens out.*

1st Nun. My lord, I ask your pardon for this haste, but death will wait for no man. My lord, as I am here, oh ! let me say a word of pleading ; of pleading for yourself, and for God's poor. 'Tis hard to think that you can be so cruel. Do you know, my lord ; your foster-mother is evicted ? Do you know that she who held you in her patient arms, through all your infancy lies dying by the wayside ? (*He starts.*) And for what crime ? The crime of poverty !

I try to think that it is your ignorance, not a hard heart brings those evils on us. Alas ! you cannot know the wrongs and frauds. Knew you your mother ? Perchance, she died while you were young and left you to the care of other hands. Perhaps your heart was never touched by mother's love. And that you cannot feel so well as those who knew it once. Could you but see the sights we see, and hear the sounds we hear, each day, no sleep nor rest would come to you till you had justice done. It is not much we ask : not even mercy, which you ask from God, but will not give to man. How will you at the last day dare to ask for mercy, when you will not give what is far less, strict justice. Your England boasts its bible; do you read it ? (*She pauses a moment.*) Put it as you will. Where do you get your daily food, but from these men ? They toil for it, with the big sweat drops on their brow. Your dainty hands, which only toil for their eviction death-warrants, are kept from labor by their toil, and then you turn and taunt them when they sink down by the wayside, broken with the work they did for you. You may stand well with the poor world, my lord, but think you, this will stand before God's angels. Oh! you know it well, but you are lying to yourself and drinking down the gall of evil. Alas ! alas ! alas ! One day you must drink deep the wormwood of regret. To-day you let these men starve, while you feast. And by a black increasement of your guilt, you lie about their state, and try to keep all help from them. And why? because you know, my lord, you are the guilty one ! You know if men in power in England knew all the truth, even they would scout you.

(LORD DRIVE-EM-OUT *mutters something to himself and turns over the leaves of a book impatiently.*)

Yes, my lord, I hear you say all this "is woman's talk." What do they know of social science, or of politics ? Perhaps not much, and yet, we know the good God made us all. And He who came to die for us has given His life for all. And we poor Sisters give our lives for those He loved so well. We do but ask that you will do a little justice to God's poor. And, if a Sister pleads, 'tis not the first time in the history of God's Church. She may be taunted, and despised, because she tells the truth. But we can bear it ! Your bible tells how Esther dared the wrath of a most cruel king to save her people. Your bible tells, how she forgot her woman's weakness in her nation's wrongs. Have you not read how Deborah ordered a battle, and how Sisera fell by woman's hand, how by God's prophet she was blessed for her brave deed. No woman's shrinking there, of freeing Israel from a tyrant; and if such deeds are not for women in these Gospel times, still more are women bound to deeds of mercy.

You talk, my lord, of men of Erin's creed, who in another land applaud your tyrannies, and condemn those who oppose them. Tell them, I pray, that Joan of Arc is all but canonized ; that of the saints who are, the holy Nun St. Catherine of Sienna stood with boldest front against oppressors. How she held sway twixt Guelph and Ghibeline, and how this Nun, bold in the strength of Heaven, withstood them all, and conquered for her God.

Such mission is not mine, but I must do my part for Erin and for God. Oh ! would, my lord, I could prevail with you to do but common justice to God's poor and to yourself. [*Exit Nuns.*

END OF FIRST ACT.

ACT II.

SCENE.—MR. HAPPYROCK *is found in a wood, felling trees. The trees can easily be represented by large stems made of brown paper. MR. HAPPYROCK has his coat off. The curtain rises on him alone felling the trunk of a tree. He pauses in the act and looks round and exclaims:*

MR. HAPPYROCK. Hard work, this. I declare, it's almost worse than dealing with the Irish landlords.

(*Enter a* SERVANT.)

SERVANT. If you please, sir; there's a deputation of Irish gentlemen— (MR. HAPPYROCK *groans audibly.*)

Before he has time to reply, or the servant to deliver his message, they crowd in, tumultuously singing "Happyrock, spare our rents." *These gentlemen are:* LORD STOPPER, *who owns large estates in the South of Ireland, and spends the rents in England;* The DUKE OF KILTENANTS, *ditto;* The EARL OF UPLANDS, *ditto;* LORD PETTY PETTY, *a nephew of the* EARL OF UPLANDS; SIR LITTLE EMLY, *an English Catholic who owns large property in Ireland, and spends most of his time in France;* SIR VERY VERY, *ditto;* LORD BAMS, *ditto, ditto; and others.*

ALL SING IN CHORUS.

AIR.—" Woodman, spare that tree."

Happyrock, spare our rents,
　　Touch not a single gale;
In '71 we stood to you,
　　And now you cannot fail.

'Twas our forefathers' axe,
   That got us all this lot
Of land in Erin, and I say,
   Your axe shall harm it not.

Those dear and precious rents,
   We spend o'er land and sea,
Say, would you cut them down
   And cause our misery.

Oft in the long ago,
   We promised to forgive
These tenants part of what they owe,
   And let the wretches live.

But we still cling to gold,
   For gold will all things bring.
Ah ! Happyrock, now hear our prayer—
   Gold is a blessed thing.

Our rents we still must have,
   So woodman harm them not.
What matter if these Irish die,
   We well can spare the lot.

Then woodman, spare our rents,
   Touch not a single gale,
And if you do, we'll stand for you,
   A peerage without fail.

SOLO.—THE DUKE OF KILTENANTS.

AIR.—" Oft in the stilly night."

Oft in these dreadful nights,
   When shots are flying round me,
Fond memory brings the light
   Of other days around me.

I think of all I used to get,
  Without a single word,
Out of my land across the sea—
  No murmurs then were heard.

But oh ! alas ! how times are changed,
  And now this wintry weather,
My agent writes to say he can't
  Get all my rents together.

Oh ! Gladstone, Gladstone, wretched man,
  What did we do to you?
That you should now undo all the past,
  And all our work undo.

Mr. Happyrock.   Well, gentlemen, and pray what is the object of this deputation ?

All.   We want our rents.

Mr. Happyrock.   I don't want to take your rents from you.
I only want you not to take everything from your unfortunate
tenants.

All.   Confiscation !   Confiscation !

Mr. Happyrock.   Well— (*he leans meditatively on his axe.*) Well,
gentlemen ; I think the less *you* say about confiscation the better.
There is not *one* of you (*he looks round sternly*) who did not get
his property by confiscation, and not so long ago, either.

(Lord Corningham *is pushed forward by the rest.*)

Lord Corningham.   Sir, these gentlemen— (*he bows obsequious-
ly right and left*) These gentlemen with me do me the honor of

asking me to speak for them, and their rents. You are perhaps aware that I am of the same religion as those unfortunate Irish.

MR. HAPPYROCK. (*Aside.*) Should not have thought it. *They* make some sacrifices for their religion ; I never heard of any *you* made yet.

LORD CORNINGHAM. They are of course an inferior race ; superstitiously attached to their religion and their priests,* but we are above that sort of thing, too highly cultivated !

MR. HAPPYROCK. (*With undisguised contempt.*) Oh ! quite so, sir; quite so, sir; I remember when the Pope made some excellent regulations lately. You showed your devotion by— ah— not accepting them. (LORD CORNINGHAM *looks confused, the others laugh.*)

LORD CORNINGHAM. But you will excuse me, my lord, if I fail to see what religion has to do with all this.* Sir, we are anxious to help you. I mean, we wish to show our loyalty to England. Those wretched Irish are so disloyal. I really do hope, sir ; you will not suppose we English Catholics take the least interest— I mean have the least affection for them. We have got all we want, and we really do not see what they want.

MR. HAPPYROCK. (*Aside, with infinite disgust.*) Of course you don't see what they want. You took care not to know, in their time of deep distress, when even Protestants felt for them and made sacrifices for them.)

Well, gentlemen ; the arrangements I propose will secure your rents ; not rack-rents certainly, but fair rents ; and if you will take an old man's advice, you will be content with fair rents. If you do not, believe me, the time is not far off when you will get no rents at all. Greed overmasters itself, and honesty is the best policy even for a landlord.

---

* A FACT.—This was said lately in the English *Catholic Tablet.*

ALL. But we want our rents. We want protection for our property. We must have trial by jury done away with.*

Mr. HAPPYROCK. I think, my lords and gentlemen, you might be satisfied with conviction for crime, and not ask for conviction for suspicion. As to you, my Lord Petty Petty, I never even heard of an outrage committed on you or your property, except your donkey's tail, and I think it was hardly necessary to get the district proclaimed in consequence, or to demand that trial by jury should be abolished in Ireland, because no one was convicted for it. But men of your class *never* learn, and I may well leave you to your fate.

As to these Catholic gentlemen, they have expressed their opinions and objections very freely. I congratulate them on their honesty and I offer them the homage of my respectful— contempt. You all have, I see, one common object—yourselves ; if you cared for England—your own country—you would care for Ireland ; and you would try by justice, fair dealing, and by the very trifling self-sacrifices necessary in a time of dire calamity to do good to England. You have made yourselves hated in Ireland ; and you have made England despised by every civilized nation, and, I am told, it was not a Protestant landlord, it was a Catholic, who in all the starvation of last year actually put a tax on the sea-snails the poor wretches were picking up off the sea-shore to keep bare life in them.†

I suspect, gentlemen, the time is past when you will be able to treat your tenants as if they were your slaves ; when you will be able to forbid them to marry ; when you will no longer be able

---

* A FACT.—The Marquis of Lansdowne brought in a Bill to the House of Lords to get the Irish jury laws altered, because the government could not get persons convicted on suspicion ! ! !

† A FACT.—Published in the London *Daily News*, and told to me by the special correspondent of the paper whom I asked was it possible it could be true. No wonder when even Catholic landlords so far forget common honesty that Ireland should be trampled on and the people enslaved by the English government. England gets bad examples from some of those who should give her the best examples if they lived up to the teaching of their holy Faith.

to double rents already oppressive by fines, and by making your tenants work for you in the harvest and the spring without payment as if they were slaves. Some of you occupy yourselves a good deal with foreign missions. I think, if you began your missions at home it would be better both for yourselves and for England.

(The deputation of landlords all take out large white pocket-hand kerchiefs and commence weeping, and with great gesticulation, turning to each other, say:)

ALL. 'Tis your fault, sir ; it's yours, my lord.

1ST VOICE. Why did you raise your rents ? Could you not have got it out of them some other way ?

2ND VOICE. Why did you sell that lime at fifty per cent above the market price ?

3RD VOICE. Why did you raise the rent for that tenant of yours because he built a house at his own expense ?

ALL. *(Cry and sob.)* Oh ! oh ! oh ! oh ! We're done ; we're undone ; we're done, oh ! oh ! What can we do ?

1ST VOICE. Let us raise the cry that the throne is in danger. Anyone refusing to pay our rack rent is trying to overthrow the throne and constitution.

2ND VOICE. Glorious constitution.

3RD VOICE. Let's go over to Rome, let's get the Pope to stop the priests ; and we will soon put down the people ; and we'll put half of them in jail and terrify the other half.

4TH VOICE. Oh ! oh ! oh ! I'm afraid the Pope won't do it. You see the Irish bishops are nearly all for the people.

(*The landlords all attack each other with threatening gestures while singing. Each sings a line or part of a line and they all join in the chorus.*)

CHORUS.

AIR.—" 'Twas you, sir; 'tis true, sir."

'Twas you, sir; 'tis true, sir,
I tell you nothing new, sir;
'Twas you that got us in this fix.
'Twas you, sir; you.

Chorus.—No, sir; no, sir;
       No, no, no, no, sir;
       'Twas you that raised the tenants' rents.
       'Twas you, sir; you.

Oh! sir; no, sir;
How can you talk up so, sir;
'Twas you put fines, sir, on the rent.
Oh! fie, sir; fie!
  No, sir; etc.

No, sir; no, sir;
I say it was not so, sir;
I only made them feed my dogs,
That could not make a row, sir.
  No, sir; etc.

No, sir; no, sir;
I am not such a fool, sir;
I only took their fowl and geese,
That should not make a stir, sir.
  No, sir; etc.

Oh, sir ; oh, sir ;
I fear we're all undone, sir ;
We don't know how this thing will end,
And we must cut and run, sir.

 No, sir ; etc.

(All run about the stage wildly.)

1ST. VOICE.	Why did you sell your lime so dear ?
2ND. VOICE.	Why did *you* raise your rent ?
3RD. VOICE.	And why, *oh ! why*, with cent per cent. Could you not be content ?

(All to each other.)

'Twas you, sir ; 'tis true, sir ;
You wanted more and more, sir ;
You bound your tenants hand and foot,
And so made all this stir, sir.

(Landlords form a half circle and continue singing and gesticulating violently at each other.)

'Twas you, sir ; 'tis true, sir ;
I tell you nothing new, sir ;
'Twas you that raised the widows' rent.
'Twas you, sir ; you.

Oh, sir ; no, sir ;
We're all in the one boat, sir ;
And we must sink or float, sir.
'Twas you, sir ; you.

END OF SECOND ACT.

ACT III.

OPENING SONG, DUETT AND CHORUS.

AIR.—" The Whistling Thief."

LANDLORD. When Pat came o'er the hill,
   Sir, I could plainly see,
  A whistle low and shrill,
   The signal was to be.
  I shouted out, police,
   Catch that young blackguard, sir.

PAT. Och ! y'er honor ; 'twas only the wind,
  Was whistling up from the sea,
  Was whistling up from the sea.

LANDLORD. You blackguard, you know the wind
   At my bidding should cease to blow,
  I've the power to loose and bind,
   All creatures here below,
   All creatures here below.

PAT. That's thrue, but you know the wind
   Mightn't know 'twas a landlord spoke,
  And faith, I think the wind,
   Knows how many a lease you broke,
   Knows how many a lease you broke.

LANDLORD. And then there's these dirty pigs,
   When I ride my bicycle down,
  Are always under my feet,
   In this dirty Irish town.

How dare these pigs to run
  In the face of an agent ? mark—
I'll have every pig of yours fined
  This night before it's dark.*

       (*Dogs bark in the distance.*)

LANDLORD.   The dogs are barking now—
         They shall bark to another tune.

PAT.   Sure, your honor, the dogs will bark,
         Whenever they see the moon,
         Whenever they see the moon.

LANDLORD.   Is it these Irish hounds,
           When they know I'm lord of the place ;
         High treason it is to bark
           In my lord or the agent's face,
           In my lord or the agent's face.

         I'm not such a fool as you think,
           I know you're a rascal, Pat,
       You shall hang, you whistling thief,
           I've made up my mind to that,
           I've made up my mind to that.

         I'll have none of these Land League tricks,
           They sha'nt play their pranks upon me ;
       I'm nearly astray in my mind,
           Myself and my family,
           Myself and my family.   [*Exit all.*

---

* A Fact.

SCENE.—*The Whistling Mite is brought into court by two very tall policemen, fully armed. He is placed in the dock, where nothing is to be seen of him, except the very top of his head.*

MR. JUSTICE (wants to be Lord Chancellor) *is on the bench and naturally wishes to please the "Fostering" government of Ireland, and the acting government—the landlord's.*

MR. WILEY (wishes to be judge Q. C.) *leads for the crown, having been retained "special," instructed by* MR. COSTS, *the crown solicitor.*

MR. FEARLESS, *who is not a Q. C., and indeed is never likely to be one, or a judge either, defends the prisoner for the Land League, instructed by* VAL. DILLON. *There is a showy bar and a long brief. Indictment is read out in court, after silence has been called by the* CRIER :

INDICTMENT.

[*Whereas*, on the (*put in the day*) in the year of (Irish) misery, 1886, the herein - named Patrick, otherwise called Pat and by his mother, *ma bouchal*, known also by the surname of *Hate the Saxon*, so-called on the maternal side, did violently, fraudulently, diabolically, traitorously, hideously, malevolently, persistently, practically, perpetually, perniciously, mercilessly, and cruelly WHISTLE in the presence of the peaceful and humane tenant-farmer-exterminator, MR. RACKRENTEM, J. P., and did thereby endanger the peace of our much-enduring lady, the queen, whose devotion to and love for her Irish subjects obliges her constantly to go to Scotland to weep in solitude over their miseries; and, *Whereas*, her peace and life is plainly aimed at by this whistling in Cork, and in fact by the existence of the Irish everywhere; and, *Whereas*, the Irish are always showing their ingratitude to her by doing something, or causing something to be done which prevents her from extending to them her royal favor, as for example; *Whereas*, of malice preforce and excited thereunto by the Land League, (the source of all evil), did compass and produce the death of her favorite and dearly beloved subject, the Earl of Baconside, at the very time that the Cork races were being carried out, so that her son, the Prince of Dublin was thereby, in consequence of the excesses of his, or her— I mean her and his grief, unable to come to the said races and was in fact obliged to run over to Paris instead, to the no small loss of her Irish subjects (and his own); and *Whereas*, the said Patrick, alias Pat, alias *ma bouchal*, alias *Hate the Saxon*, has done a most serious and malignant injury to her most devoted-to-Ireland Majesty the Queen, thereby endangering the loss of her patronage and affection for that wicked and ungrateful people; and, *Whereas*, the said Patrick, alias Pat, alias *Hate the Saxon*, has committed the fearful outrage and ingratitude of whistling at the aforesaid MR. RACKRENTEM, J. P., thereby causing him great mental perturbation, and placing him in great physical fear, and inducing heart disease, a disease hitherto unknown to that gentleman, he not having been previously aware that he had such an organ; and *Whereas*, he feels, and has been made to feel, mortal terror in consequence of the outrage committed on him by the said Pat, so that it may be truly said of him :

> My hair was grey,
> It now is white,
> It turned a shade
> With this terrible fright ;

and, *Whereas*, he has suffered severely in his vocal organs, from the exertion of calling the police to rescue him from this Pat or Patrick. The police being always and generally never at the place where they are most wanted. The said Pat is to be tried by an uncommon jury selected by the landlord protectors of Ireland.

(*The* CRIER *bows to the* JUDGE.)

THE JUDGE. Call the jury panel, sir.

CRIER. Tim O'Sullivan.

TIM O'SULLIVAN. Here, sir

MR. WANTS-TO-BE-JUDGE Q. C. (*objects*) Tim is a member of the Land League, my lord.

JUDGE. (*Seriously addressing* TIM.) Go down, sir; you ought to be ashamed of yourself, sir; Land League, indeed. I'll make a Land League of you, and land you into Kilmainham jail, sir.

CRIER. Thomas Brownrigg.

THOMAS BROWNRIGG. Here, sir.

MR. FEARLESS. I object, my lord. He is rent-warner to LORD EVICTEM, and he would soon be evicted himself, if he gave evidence according to his conscience.

JUDGE. Nonsense, sir; nonsense. LORD EVICTEM is a most respectable gentleman.

(THOMAS BROWNRIGG *is made foreman of the jury.*)

CRIER. James McCarthy.

JAMES McCARTHY. Here, sir.

MR. WANTS-TO-BE-JUDGE. I object, my lord. His lordship sent some of his hounds to this fellow to rear for him and he had the impudence to say he wanted every drop of milk he had for his children.

JUDGE. Stand down, sir; you are quite unfit for the severe responsibility of such a case as this.

CRIER. John Mahoney.

JOHN MAHONEY. Here, sir.

Mr. Wants-to-be-Judge. (*Hurriedly whispers to* **Judge.**) Pass him, my lord ; pass him. He is a souper— I, ahem— I mean, he is a good Protestant.

Mr. Fearless. My lord, I object.

Judge. Sir, you have no business to object. Next time, sir; I presume, you will object to *me.*

Voice in the Crowd. Faith and he might do worse.

Judge. Silence, sir. Crier, see that the court is cleared. Put out every one; every one, I say, sir.

Voice in the Crowd. Faith, my lord ; that's just what we want. If ye'd only begin with putting yourself out first.

Judge. Hold your tongue, sir. Crier, I will report you, sir. Police, arrest that man.

Policeman. Which man, my lord ?

Judge. Silence, sir ; no one asked you to speak. (*Addresses the crowd.*) I will make a clean sweep of this court if one more word is said in it.

Mr. Wants-etc. My lord—

A shout in the Crowd. Take him up, arrest him, policeman. (*A long, loud whistle.*) Hurray boys. (*General confusion.*)

(**Pat,** *wishing to see the fun, peers out over the box and holds on with both hands so as to raise his head up over it.*)

Judge. Policeman, turn that boy out instantly.

Policeman. (*Respectfully.*) Which boy, my lord ?

JUDGE. Put him out, I say. Am I to get no respect here— even from the servants of the queen? Little boys of his age should not be allowed into such a place.

VOICE IN THE CROWD. Thrue for your honor's worship.

BOY'S MOTHER IN THE CROWD. Ah! thin, come to your mother, *nut bouchal;* there's his honor's letting you off.

POLICEMAN. My lord, this boy is the prisoner.

JUDGE. (*Whistles*) Why cannot I see him, sir? Tell him to stand up, sir. I will not be treated this way!

POLICEMAN. My lord— Please your lordship, he can't stand up— I mean— he is standing up.

VOICE IN THE CROWD. God save Ireland!

CHORUS (*outside of Court House*).

Oh! such a wretched country
    As this was never seen,
For they're trying all our little boys,
    For whistling on the green,
    For whistling on the green.
For they're trying all our little boys,
    For whistling on the green.

(*The* JUDGE *leans back in his seat and lifts up his hands and eyes in pious grief.*)

POLICEMAN. My lord, he is very small. He can't help it, my lord.

VOICE IN THE CROWD. Ah! thin, policeman, darlin', comb up his hair. Here's a comb, your honor. And sure, if you'd make it stand up straight, his honor's worship could see the hair of his head, anyway.

JUDGE. (*Sternly to* MR. WANTS-etc.) Go on with your case, sir.

MR. WANTS-etc. My lord, the prisoner at the bar— I mean the child in the box— has been charged with the awful crime of whistling, and of whistling at a landlord. The words in the indictment are defamatory. Imagine, my lord, and gentlemen of the jury— (*pauses*). My lord, I believe we have not got a jury, after all, but it does not matter. They are sure not to convict, and your lordship can pass sentence all the same—

VOICE IN THE CROWD. Glory be to God, and sure he can. God help us it would be poor law if we'd be thried this way at the Day of Judgment.

Mr. WANTS-etc. Of course, in a country like this, my lord; the law is habitually set at defiance—

VOICE IN THE CROWD. Och! thin ; but it's thrue for ye. Sure it's all agin the poor, and all for the rich. Och ! but y'er the good gentleman entirely, entirely—

JUDGE. Go on, sir ; go on. Don't mind interruptions. It doesn't matter ; in fact, nothing matters. (*He settles himself to sleep.*)

Mr. WANTS-etc. After your lordships profound remarks, which show such a high appreciation of law and justice, I will continue, though my words, I fear are super—fluous.

This person— I mean—ahem— this young boy, requires a serious lesson to sober him for life, and to teach him his duty in that state of life in which the English government has been pleased to place him. He must, indeed, be a dreadful, and a very hardened little boy, to have so terrified such a very nice gentleman ; to have produced in him a heart to beat for his own woes, if not for the woes of other people. My lord, if the hearts of Irish landlords, I mean, of course, if the landlords of Irish hearts, are to be affected in this way, the sooner her most gracious majesty the queen is advised to give up the crown and constitution the better. In fact, no constitution could stand this kind of work, and the only crown we would have would be a half crown. It is fearful to think what one wicked little boy can do.

(Little boy's head just looks over the box and pops down again.)

Mr. Wants-etc. My lord, as I was saying, when that bad boy looked at me, if the hearts of Irish landlords are to be affected in this way— I tremble— I tremble, to think of the consequences. *(He turns to the boy.)* Little boy, you have affected the heart of an Irish landlord. It is a physiological phenomenon to find a heart in such a quarter. In fact, the hearts of Irish landlords have been so frequently evicted by their owners and when not evicted so completely ossified from want of action that it was cruel to awake them. Indeed the words of the poet Moore might well be addressed to them,

> I'd mourn the hopes that leave me,
> If my rents had left me too,
> But while I keep my purse well filled,
> I can steel my heart anew—

and so on, in fact, my lord ; a treatise has been written on the whole subject of the hearts of Irish landlords, by the late Mr. Cromwell and the revered Mr. Froude to both of whom, embraced in each others arms, a statue should be erected in Dublin. Indeed speaking of statues in Dublin, I understand the statue of justice placed at the Castle gates has its face turned away from the people* and that it is proposed to signalize the passing of this Bill for the protection of the lives and properties of Irish landlords by placing a statue of justice upside down in the law courts. I would also advise that a cast of this little boy should be taken before he is cast into jail, and kept to be handed down to posterity

---

* A Fact.

for the benefit of his ancestors— I mean, of course, of his great grand-children's ancestors, to show how little boys behaved in this nineteenth century to their good and loving landlords. My lord, tears ought to flow. (*Aside.* I am sorry to say mine won't for LORD DRIVE-EM-OUT is looking at me) when one thinks of what a pretty pass things have come to in Ireland. I am grieved, my lord, that an unkind Providence caused me to be born in this unhappy country, which I can plainly see exists only that I may sell it and sever myself from it. I have digressed, my lord; but I return to our original matter, or rather to the little lamb before us. When I was a little boy—

VOICE IN THE CROWD. Faith and sure you were a beauty.

ANOTHER VOICE. I don't think it was milk his mother fed him on.

JUDGE. (*Tries to look resigned to anything.*) Go on, sir; go on. It doesn't matter; in fact, nothing matters.

MR. WANTS-etc. My lord— my lord, I go back to the time when I was a little boy—

MR. FEARLESS. My lord, is it necessary for counsel to go into the history of his early years?

JUDGE. (*Angry at being woke up, having just settled himself for a quiet doze.*) Whose early years, sir? I know nothing about early years, I had no early years, sir. (*To counsel.*) Go on, sir; go on, sir; it does'nt matter; in fact, nothing matters.

MR. WANTS-etc. As I was saying, my lord, when I met this unseemly interruption to my early years—when I was young—

(*Voice in the crowd, singing softly.*)

When I was young I had no sense,
  I bought a fiddle for eighteen pence,
And all the tune that I could play, was
    Get the landlords out of my way,
    Och ! get the landlords out of my way.

(*Judge slumbers peacefully.*)

Mr. Wants-etc. (*Counsel folds his arms and addresses the crowd generally.*) Very good, gentlemen, very good. When you are *quite* finished singing, I'll go on.

Voice in the Crowd. Och, go on, yer honor; yer doing it illegant.

Mr. Wants-etc. In my early years—

Judge. (*Waking up.*) Ahem. What, sir; I think— ahem— you might have got over your early years, sir. I never had any, sir; but it does not matter; in fact, nothing matters. (*Settles himself to sleep again.*)

Mr. Wants-etc. This little boy, my lord—

Judge. I thought, sir; we had got past your boyhood's days—

Voice in the Crowd. Thrue for ye, yer honor. Faith, he's past them long ago.

2nd Voice. Och, sure, he never began 'em.

Judge. (*Now thoroughly aroused, and very angry.*) Silence, every one of you. What use are the police ?

Voice in the crowd. To court the girls, ye'r honour.

2nd Voice. That's over anyway; the girls won't look at them, now they're doing the dirty work for the landlords.

Judge. I'll stop the trial, sir. I'll bring the horse marines down here— I mean the cavalry and fill the place with them next time I come to the assizes. I'll finish the case now myself.

MR. FEARLESS. My lord, surely you will allow me to address the court for the prisoner.

JUDGE. I will not, sir. I'll not allow any addresses, sir. Too many addresses already from the Land League, sir. Stand down, sir— I mean, sit up, sir— but it doesn't matter ; in fact, nothing matters. Policeman, hold up that little boy, I mean the prisoner, sir.

VOICE IN THE CROWD. His mother'll hould him in her arms ye'r honor, while you're passing the sentence to let him off.

JUDGE. Policeman put him on his head— I mean of course, let me see his head,— but it doesn't matter ; in fact, nothing matters. (*Addresses the boy, who is held up by his arms by two policemen.*) Little boy, in the box, I mean, prisoner at the bar, you have, in fact, placed a bar to all your farther proceedings in life by your barbarous conduct to this gentleman, a humane tenant-farmer-exterminator, MR. RACKRENTEM. Why little boys like you were ever born is a puzzle which I leave to— ahem,— Mr. Darwin. In fact, why little boys are born at all in Ireland is a puzzle, because, as a very eminent and distinguished statistician observed the other day, if there were no little boys in Ireland there would be no men, and then our— I mean the English government would not have the trouble of making laws for their extermination— I mean, of course, emigration, but it doesn't matter; in fact—ahem—nothing matters. Little boy, I really don't know what is to be done with you. If you had not been born— I mean, of course, if you had been born in England you would not have been Irish, and everything would have been different. Little English boys don't commit such— ahem— trifling crimes, they do something for which a judge *can* sentence them. It really is quite too absurd to be obliged to pass sentence on what I may be permitted to call a penny whistle. Why, little boy, were you born, and why, little boy, having been born, did you whistle ? A little English boy, not much older than you are, was tried the other day for murdering his mistress ; that was what I might call a sensible crime— I mean, of course, a sentenceable one, but it doesn't matter ; in fact, nothing matters. He wasn't convicted. There being only a "reasonable suspicion" of his guilt. In England, of course, this was no failure of justice, as neither boys nor men are allowed to be punished unless their guilt is made quite clear. In Ireland, it is happily different. The kind and fostering government under which you are placed has arranged otherwise. In fact, your foster-father has quite taken the place —*locus parentis*—counsel will understand me—of your natural guardians, or rather of your legal guardians, and altogether deprived you of English law which, of course, was never intended for you. This thoughtful and parental care has, I fear, been lost upon you. In Ireland, little boy, as you probably know, suspicion reasonable or unreasonable is quite sufficient. Such is the benevolence of your government— I mean, of course, of the way in which you are governed, but it doesn't matter ; in fact, nothing matters. Your father, I am told, by the gentleman whom you so cruelly insulted, has been the object of this special parental attention on the part of your good English foster-father. Oh ! little boy, I am ashamed of you ! I grieve for you— I weep to think of it. This excellent gentleman assured the priest of your parish, before the act for the protection of his life and property was passed that if all his tenants did not pay rents* he would take care the act should be put in force against them, and if they did pay him he would take care they should not suffer thereby. This was, of course, most humane on his part, but I regret to say, I deeply regret to say his humanity was not appreciated as it should have been. Your father actually refused to pay his rent. In fact, he had the insolence to say he had not got it. Two of his cows, he said, had died, and his daughter in America who had sent home money every year before to help to pay the rent, was ill. I would like to know how he dare offer such excuses. Why should his cows have died more than anyone else's cows, and why should his daughter have been ill. It is a— ahem— rascally outrage, and a specimen of the way in which Irish tenants are always excusing themselves, when asked to pay their lawful debts. Your father was very properly arrested on suspicion. If he did not intend to refuse to pay his rent, he probably would have in-

---

* A FACT. See Appendix.

tended it at some future time, and your good and kind landlords are now gifted with the power (once supposed to be only divine) of seeing into your most inmost thoughts, and then of "suspecting" what you intend, or may at some future time intend to do. Hence all this care of you—in fact, the only thing you have any right to intend to do in Ireland is to intend to emigrate, and the sooner you do that the better. Every one should emigrate. There are twice too many people in the country already. Why some of you were born has always been an inexplicable mystery to me. You might have known, in fact,— ahem— you should have known you were not wanted. You are in the way of— of everybody, in fact, there is not a landlord in Ireland who has not said repeatedly that they could get on better without you. It has, indeed, sometimes occurred to myself that there might be a difficulty in cultivating the land if there was no one to do it, and that— ahem— in fact, if you all left in a body nobody would remain, but they don't seem to see it somehow, but it doesn't matter ; in fact— ahem— nothing matters. Only I suppose if you all left, it would remove a great social difficulty, and, in fact, save your kind and good landlords a deal of trouble. They would, I suppose, import Chinese, for it does seem to me that some kind of rent-producing machine would be required. You, as far as I can learn, would go farther and fare better. Why then, in the name of heaven, don't you go and leave the country, where you had no business to be born, and which you certainly have no business to live in. I hear some one say something about providence putting you here. Quite a mistake, sir. We have nothing to do with providence. All that is given up in England, long ago. The— ahem— greatest good of the smallest number is the great lesson of modern science. For example, if you, little boy, had never been born, you would not be where you are, but being born, unfortunately, the one thing to do is to get you somewhere else as quickly as possible. Under ordinary circumstances I would have recommended a forcible application of the— ahem— maternal slipper, as the fittest punishment for your crime, but unfortunately your mother has no slipper ; in fact, she has not a sole to her heel, another evidence of the lamentable depravity of the Irish race. Why Irish women do not wear shoes and stockings is beyond my comprehension. All the women and little girls do in England, but then, of course, England is not Ireland, and it does not matter ; in fact, nothing matters.

But, little boy, to return to you. I am lost in amazement at your ingratitude. How could you whistle at your good and kind landlord ? Don't you know, little boy, when there was said to be some—ahem—distress last year, he made the very best of it for you by writing to the English papers to say it didn't exist, and that, if it did, it really didn't matter ; in fact, that nothing matters ; except, of course, making you do your duty in life : to pay your rents. What more could he have done for you, except, indeed, to give you food, or encourage other people to give it to you ; but that would have been bad for you, in fact, quite demoralizing. At the same time, he gave £1,000 towards the election expenses of a friend in England. As he is naturally anxious to have you properly represented in the English parliament, and as gentlemen who have never been in Ireland are the most suited for that purpose, as, knowing nothing, they cannot be prejudiced in your favor. Prejudice, little boy, is very wicked, and nothing but prejudice could cause your wicked whistling. Then, you know, little boy, how your landlord brought over a number of clever gentlemen from England to see how well off you were, and how happy and contented ; and one gentleman from France, who, as he could not understand one word of English, was of course a great deal more likely to understand the Irish question. Then, knowing there is nothing half so good for a struggling man as to raise his rent, he took the opportunity of doing so, and having borrowed money very cheaply from government ; he employed you at your own expense, and kindly made you pay for it after by raising your rent, and told his English friends there was no manure for land so good as Raising the Rent.

(*Loud shouts outside.—Singing, cheering, etc.*)

Voice. (*Shouts out.*) Cable message just arrived. Ireland Free ! ! ! Mr. Gladstone's Bill to give Ireland a Parliament of her own passed by tremendous majority ! .

END.

OPENING SONG AND CHORUS.

I WISH YOU THE TOP OF THE MORNING.

My heart's dear love, but there it is—

The dawn ou the hills of Ireland— God's an-gel's lift - ing

the night's black veil, From the fair sweet face of my sire-land!

O Ire-land, isn't it grand you look, Like a bride in

her rich a - dorn-ing. And with all the pent up love

of my heart— I wish you the top of the morning.

CHORUS, single voices.

I wish you the top of the morning— I wish you the

top of the morning. Oh!.......... Ire - land dear,

repeat chorus with all the voices.

don't you hear me shout, I wish you the top of the morning.

2.

This one short hour pays lavishly back,
  For many a year of mourning ;
I'd almost venture another flight,
  There's so much joy in returning ;
Watching out for the hallowed shore,
  All other attractions scornin' !

I wish you the top o' the mornin' !
I wish you the top o' the mornin' !
O Ireland, dear ! don't you hear me shout !
I wish you the top o' the mornin' !

3.

Ho ! ho ! upon Cleena's shelving strand,
  The surges are grandly beating,
And Kerry is pushing her headlands out
  To give us the kindly greeting ;
Into the shore the sea-birds fly,
  On pinions that know no drooping ;
And out from the cliffs, with welcomes charged,
  A million of waves come trooping.

I wish you the top o' the mornin' !
I wish you the top o' the mornin' !
O Ireland, dear ! don't you hear me shout !
I wish you the top o' the mornin' !

4.

O kindly, generous, Irish land,
  So leal, and fair, and loving,
No wonder the wandering Celt should think
  And dream of you in his roving !

The alien home may have gems and gold,
  Shadows may never have gloomed it ;
But the heart will sigh for the absent land,
  Where the love-light first illumed it.

  I wish you the top o' the mornin' !
   I wish you the top o' the mornin' !
O Ireland, dear ! don't you hear me shout !
  I wish you the top o' the mornin' !

5.

And doesn't t' old Cove look charming there,
  Watching the wild wave's motion,
Leaning her back up against the hills,
  And the top of her toes on the ocean.
I wonder I don't hear Shandon's bells,
  Ah ! maybe their chiming's over,
For it's many a year since I began
  The life of a western rover.

  I wish you the top o' the mornin' !
  I wish you the top o' the mornin' !
O Ireland, dear ! don't you hear me shout !
  I wish you the top o' the mornin' !

6.

For thirty summers, astore machree,
  Those hills I now feast my eyes on
Ne'er met my vision save when they rose
  Over memory's dim horizon.
E'en so 'twas grand and fair they seemed,
  In the landscape spread before me.
But dreams are dreams, and my eyes would ope,
  To see Texas' sky still o'er me.

  I wish you the top o' the mornin' !
  I wish you the top o' the mornin' !
O Ireland, dear ! don't you hear me shout !
  I wish you the top o' the mornin' !

7.

Ah ! often upon the Texan plain,
  When the day and the chase were over,
My thoughts would fly o'er the weary wave,
  And around this coast-line hover.
And the prayer would rise that some future day,
  All danger and doubtings scornin',
I'd help to win for my native land
  The light of young liberty's mornin'.

  I wish you the top o' the mornin' !
  I wish you the top o' the mornin' !
O Ireland, dear ! don't you hear me shout !
  I wish you the top o' the mornin' !

8.

Now fuller and truer the shore-line shows—
  Was ever a scene so splendid ?
I feel the breath of the Munster breeze ;
  Thank God that my exile's ended.
Old scenes, old songs, old friends again,
  The vale and cot I was born in !
O Ireland, up from my heart of hearts,
  I wish you the top o' the mornin' !

  I wish you the top o' the mornin' !
  I wish you the top o' the mornin' !
O Ireland, dear ! don't you hear me shout !
  I wish you the top o' the mornin' !

APPENDIX.

APPENDIX.

It may be thought that one part of this play is severe on English Catholics. To condemn them *en masse* would be as unjust as most universal condemnations are. But there is no doubt, in fact, there is very ample proof, that English Catholics have not taken the practical interest in the welfare of Irish Catholics to which even the interest of a common religion should have bound them. The cause of this is not far to seek. A pamphlet has been published lately in England bearing the title "We Catholics," it has had a very large circulation, possibly because of its profuse laudations of certain literary English Catholics. It might be supposed, indeed, from the fulsome dedication to a Mr. Cox, that English Catholics were the only Catholics of any account in the Universal Church, and that Mr. Cox was destined to be their prophet. The author addresses him thus : "Versed in the wisdom of the world, you inherit besides, and, I will add, you illustrate the traditions of Fidelity to the Faith handed down to you from your own fathers, and by your mother, from the Welds, and I see in you a future Publicist to whom is open the happy possibility of restoring to our community that *esprit de corps* for which I venture in the following pages to plead."

The last sentence is the key note of the pamphlet. But in what is this *esprit de corps* made to consist, which is to accomplish such wonders for [English] Catholics ? Apparently it is to form a Mutual Admiration Society as a bond to keep "We [English] Catholics" together. How poor is all this in the face of the real and terrible dangers of worldliness which are the true evils to be feared, especially by English Catholics, whose social position has gained an advance which may be far more dangerous to their interests than they at present suppose ; but *not one* word is said in the pamphlet, from cover to cover, on the subject of Irish Catholics. They are as completely ignored as if no such persons existed. Certainly, with all reverence I say it, this was not the *esprit de corps* of the Apostles, or of the early Christians. I am afraid Lord Kenmare hardly likes to be called an Irish Catholic, but he is one all the same, and he is singled out for special attack by the author of this flowery pamphlet. And for what ? Simply because the anonymous writer thinks that Lord Kenmare licensed some plays which were not up to his standard of morality. On this subject I express no opinion, as I am entirely and happily ignorant as to the grounds of this charge.

But why has this person nothing to say of Lord Kenmare's treatment of his Irish tenants ? Are they so altogether out of the paths of grace, or civilization, as to be refused admission to the wonderful " We " ? Are these Irish tenants not Catholics, as well as the great English " We," who are so earnestly urged to praise one another ? Writing of Lord Kenmare, the author of " We Catholics " says : " Sister M. Francis Clare is said to be in want of a Mission ; and I therefore venture to propose to her one which only the possession of undaunted energy would allow her to undertake, and which at the same time gives grounds for the continuance of her title, The Nun of Kenmare. Having left the town, let her devote herself to the Earl of that ilk ; and by letters, pamphlets, and the pastorals of friendly Bishops, endeavor to arouse the moral consciousness of the department of the Lord Chamberlain ! "

This curiously written sentence contains as many false statements as there are lines, and it gives evidence, if evidence were needed, how little English Catholics care even to know the simplest matter about Irish affairs.

Sister M. Francis Clare is not in want of a Mission. She has a noble one given to her by the Head of the Holy Catholic Church, and if the opposition of " We Catholics," of the type of this writer has prevented her for a time, at least, from carrying it out in Ireland, their power is limited by the holy will of God, and she will work, and is working for her people elsewhere.

Her mission certainly was not pleasing to certain English Catholics who own large property in Ireland for very obvious reasons. If her reports given to the whole world through the Press were true, her statement that poor Irish Catholics were not treated by their English Catholic landlords with that *esprit de corps* which the Apostles preached to the early Christians, it is little wonder that her mission was very distasteful to them.

It would be an insult if it was not too great an absurdity to suggest that the Nun of Kenmare would occupy herself by writing "letters, pamphlets, and the pastorals of friendly Bishops, endeavor to arouse the moral consciousness of the department of the Lord Chamberlain ! " or whatever this curiously constructed sentence may mean.

One of the most beloved and truly patriotic Archbishops of America whose letter is now before us, has given the true cause why the Nun of Kenmare has had the misfortune to displease "We Catholics," and further this prelate has written from personal and accurate knowledge : as he was in Ireland at the time. In a letter to the Very Rev. Canon B———, his grace says : " A very sad news has reached me that the good Sister Mary Francis Clare had to leave Knock, and her Convent unfinished, owing to the opposition of ——— and that the Providence of God has opened a door for her in England by the good Bishop of Nottingham who even vacated his own house for the good Nun, whose efforts in Ireland were so thwarted. God help poor Ireland !

"She is a lady of very great intellect, of large mind, and large heart, exceedingly charitable to the poor, loved her country earnestly, perhaps too much for the tastes of her opponents. The government and landlords may now rejoice, that they got rid of one who so ably exposed their crimes and wickedness. Of course she won't have the same occasion to write in England as she has had in Ireland.

"Many a good and religious patriotic heart will weep over this sad stroke to Ireland and Knock, as Christ wept over Jerusalem."

The author of "We Catholics" is as ignorant of Irish affairs as he is of what has been done in Rome to enable the Nun of Kenmare to establish her Mission of Peace. The town of Kenmare is not on the property of Lord Kenmare. We believe he obtains his title from a little village of the same name near Limerick.

The town of Kenmare and the surrounding districts belong to the Marquis of Lansdowne, the present Governor-General of Canada, and one of the most active exterminators of the Irish race by emigration.

The following extracts from a "Report of the English Miners' Delegation to Kerry" will show that the Marquis of Lansdowne was as much interested in the Nun of Kenmare's leaving Ireland as any of the many landlords whose unhappy tenants she was the means of saving from starvation:

"There are few, indeed, as well acquainted with the causes of the present condition of this country as Sister Mary Francis Clare, the world-famed Nun of Kenmare. Her life has been devoted to the study of the history of the nation, to the examination of the idiosyncracies, the customs, and the aspirations of the people, and her writings on these subjects have a recognized importance which puts them beyond the reach of our humble encomium. We would, therefore, have been guilty of an unpardonable breach of duty had we passed through Kenmare without calling on the lady whose charity and genius have made the name of this hamlet a household word among all civilized nations. There was fearful distress in and around Kenmare during 1879, and Sister Mary Francis Clare did all she possibly could to alleviate it. While she was thus making the most bitter sacrifices to save the people from starvation, Lord Lansdowne and his agent Mr. Trench, were doing all they could to counteract her influence and stop charitably-disposed persons from giving subscriptions. It would seem that it suited Lord Lansdowne's purpose to deny that any body on his estate was suffering any hardship whatever, and, that whoever was so positioned, it was through thriftlessness or laziness. Distress is chronic here, and last week a deputation of laborers came to Sister Mary Francis Clare, at the Convent, seeking for employment. They represented about fifty families, and having got little or no work or food for some weeks, they were in a state of desperation. There were then some public works in the neighborhood to be done for which a government loan had been obtained, and there had been some delay in opening them. The Sister at once telegraphed to the gentleman who had charge of these works, telling him that if they were not opened in twenty-four hours, she would have the matter brought before Parliament. She got a reply to the effect that they would be opened in twenty-four hours. In the meantime she set the men to work at little jobs at one shilling and six pence per day, but at the same time she did not know how she would get the money to pay them. 'Go to work,' she said to them, 'and God will provide your wages.' The next morning she received a letter from the Viceroy of India, the Marquis of Ripon, enclosing a check for £10.

During the period over which the distress continued in Ireland, the Nun of Kenmare distributed in various parts of the country £15,000 which had been sent to her from all parts of the world."

www.ingramcontent.com/pod-product-compliance
Lightning Source LLC
Chambersburg PA
CBHW031321280626
47169CB00019B/2569